A Note to Parents

Welcome to REAL KIDS READERS, a series of phonics-based books for children who are beginning to read. In the classroom, educators use phonics to teach children how to sound out unfamiliar words, providing a firm foundation for reading skills. At home, you can use REAL KIDS READERS to reinforce and build on that foundation, because the books follow the same basic phonic guidelines that children learn in school.

Of course the best way to help your child become a good reader is to make the experience fun—and REAL KIDS READERS do that, too. With their realistic story lines and lively characters, the books engage children's imaginations. With their clean design and sparkling photographs, they provide picture clues that help new readers decipher the text. The combination is sure to entertain young children and make them truly want to read.

REAL KIDS READERS have been developed at three distinct levels to make it easy for children to read at their own pace.

- LEVEL 1 is for children who are just beginning to read.
- LEVEL 2 is for children who can read with help.
- LEVEL 3 is for children who can read on their own.

A controlled vocabulary provides the framework at each level. Repetition, rhyme, and humor help increase word skills. Because children can understand the words and follow the stories, they quickly develop confidence. They go back to each book again and again, increasing their proficiency and sense of accomplishment, until they're ready to move on to the next level. The result is a rich and rewarding experience that will help them develop a lifelong love of reading.

For Ariel,
a winner in anybody's book
—C. S.

For Simone and Finn
—D. H.

Special thanks to Raynor Suter Hardware, Mattituck, NY,
and to Julianna Carlson.

Produced by DWAI / Seventeenth Street Productions, Inc.
Reading Specialist: Virginia Grant Clammer

Millbrook Press, Inc.
A division of Lerner Publishing Group
241 First Avenue North
Minneapolis, MN 55401 U.S.A.

Website address: www.lernerbooks.com

Library of Congress Cataloging-in-Publication Data

Simon, Charnan.
   I like to win! / Charnan Simon ; photographs by Dorothy Handelman.
       p.   cm. — (Real kids readers. Level 1)
   Summary: Trouble arises between a brother and sister because she always wins the games they play, but then she discovers that she does not have to brag or win all the time.
   ISBN-13: 978–0–7613–2062–3 (lib. bdg. : alk. paper)
   ISBN-10: 0–7613–2062–8 (lib. bdg. : alk. paper)
   ISBN-13: 978–0–7613–2087–6 (pbk. : alk. paper)
   ISBN-10: 0–7613–2087–3 (pbk. : alk. paper)
   [1. Winning and losing—Fiction. 2. Brothers and sisters—Fiction. 3. Stories in rhyme.]
I. Handelman, Dorothy, ill. II. Title. III. Series.
PZ8.3.S5874Il   1999
[E]—dc21
                                            98-56273

Manufactured in the United States of America
5 6 7 8 9 10 – DP – 11 10 09 08 07 06

I Like to Win!

By Charnan Simon
Photographs by Dorothy Handelman

M Millbrook Press • Minneapolis

I like to win!

And when we play,
I win a lot.
It makes my day.

I like to win!
I run so fast.

9

I do not miss . . .

or come in last.

But what is this?
Now you are mad?

You will not play?

That makes me sad.

You will not play?
That can not be!

It is not fun
when it's just me.

We make a plan.

Now when we play,
you don't get mad
or run away.

I do not yell
or brag to you.

I like to win—
and you do too!

Reading with Your Child

1. Try to read with your child at least twenty minutes each day, as part of your regular routine.
2. Keep your child's books in one convenient, cozy reading spot.
3. Read and familiarize yourself with the Phonic Guidelines below.
4. Ask your child to read *I Like to Win* out loud. If he or she has difficulty with a word:
   • Help him or her decode the word phonetically. (Say, "Try to sound it out.")
   • Encourage him or her to use picture clues. (Say, "What does the picture show?")
   • Ask him or her to use context clues. (Say, "What would make sense?")
5. If your child still doesn't "get" the word, tell him or her what it is. Don't wait for frustration to build.
6. Praise your beginning reader. With your enthusiasm and encouragement, your child will go from one success to the next.

Phonic Guidelines

Use the following guidelines to help your child read the words in *I Like to Win*.

Short Vowels

When two consonants surround a vowel, the sound of the vowel is usually short. This means you pronounce *a* as in apple, *e* as in egg, *i* as in igloo, *o* as in octopus, and *u* as in umbrella. Short-vowel words in this story include: *but, can, fun, get, lot, mad, not, run, sad, win.*

Short-Vowel Words with Beginning Consonant Blends

When two different consonants begin a word, they usually blend to make a combined sound. Words in this story with beginning consonant blends include: *brag, plan.*

Short-Vowel Words with Ending Consonant Blends

When two different consonants end a word, they usually blend to make a combined sound. Words in this story with ending consonant blends include: *fast, just, last.*

Double Consonants

When two identical consonants appear side by side, one of them is silent. In this story, double consonants appear in the short-vowel words *miss, will,* and *yell.*

Sight Words

Sight words are those words that a reader must learn to recognize immediately—by sight—instead of by sounding them out. They occur with high frequency in easy texts. Sight words not included in the above categories are: *a, and, are, be, come, day, do, I, in, is, it, like, make, me, my, now, or, play, so, that, this, to, too, we, what, when, you.*